CHRISTMAS AT
THE KEEP

For more information on Marcia Willett and her books,
see her website at www.marciawillett.co.uk

CHRISTMAS AT THE KEEP

MARCIA WILLETT

BANTAM PRESS

TRANSWORLD PUBLISHERS
Penguin Random House, One Embassy Gardens,
8 Viaduct Gardens, London SW11 7BW
www.penguin.co.uk

Transworld is part of the Penguin Random House group of companies
whose addresses can be found at global.penguinrandomhouse.com

First published in Great Britain in 2022 by Bantam Press
an imprint of Transworld Publishers

A CIP catalogue record for this book
is available from the British Library.

ISBN 9781787633230

Typeset in 13.25/18.5 pt Fournier MT Pro by Jouve (UK), Milton Keynes
Printed and bound in Great Britain by Clays Ltd, Elcograf S.p.A.

The authorized representative in the EEA is Penguin Random House Ireland,
Morrison Chambers, 32 Nassau Street, Dublin D02 YH68.

Penguin Random House is committed to a sustainable future
for our business, our readers and our planet. This book is made
from Forest Stewardship Council® certified paper.

To Charles

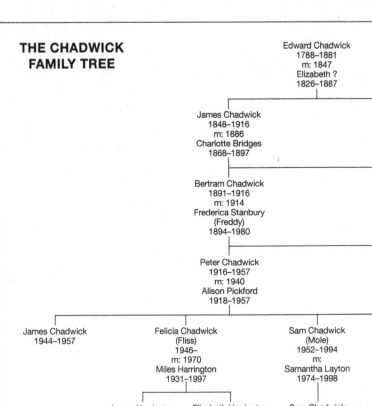

THE CHADWICK FAMILY TREE

Edward Chadwick
1788–1881
m: 1847
Elizabeth ?
1826–1887

James Chadwick
1848–1916
m: 1886
Charlotte Bridges
1868–1897

Bertram Chadwick
1891–1916
m: 1914
Frederica Stanbury
(Freddy)
1894–1980

Peter Chadwick
1916–1957
m: 1940
Alison Pickford
1918–1957

James Chadwick
1944–1957

Felicia Chadwick
(Fliss)
1946–
m: 1970
Miles Harrington
1931–1997

Sam Chadwick
(Mole)
1952–1994
m:
Samantha Layton
1974–1998

James Harrington
1973–

Elizabeth Harrington
(Bess)
1973–
m: 1995
Matthew Foster

Sam Chadwick
1995–

Paula Foster
1997–

Timmy Foster
2002–

NOTES:
Maria Chadwick marries Adam Wishart (1948–2006) in 1995 following her divorce from Henry Chadwick.

Henry (Hal) Chadwick and Felicia (Fliss) Harrington marry in 1998.

Full details may be found in The Chadwick Trilogy: *Looking Forward*, *Holding On* and *Winning Through*, and also in *The Prodigal Wife*.

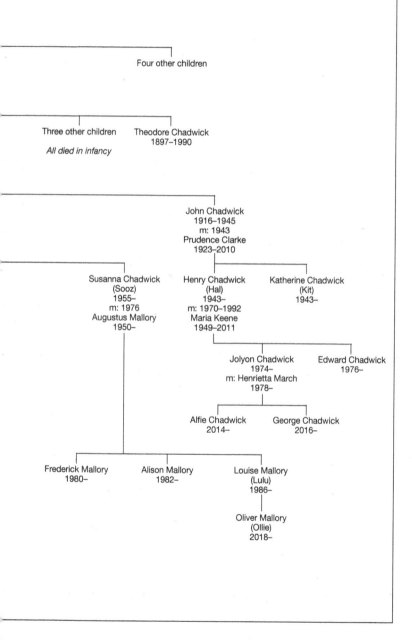

Four other children

Three other children   Theodore Chadwick
                                    1897–1990

All died in infancy

John Chadwick
1916–1945
m: 1943
Prudence Clarke
1923–2010

Susanna Chadwick   Henry Chadwick   Katherine Chadwick
(Sooz)   (Hal)   (Kit)
1955–   1943–   1943–
m: 1976   m: 1970–1992
Augustus Mallory   Maria Keene
1950–   1949–2011

Jolyon Chadwick   Edward Chadwick
1974–   1976–
m: Henrietta March
1978–

Alfie Chadwick   George Chadwick
2014–   2016–

Frederick Mallory   Alison Mallory   Louise Mallory
1980–   1982–   (Lulu)
                                                     1986–

Oliver Mallory
(Ollie)
2018–

CHAPTER ONE

October

'Ed's coming home.'

There is a little silence. Hal Chadwick puts his iPhone on the kitchen table and looks at Fliss. Ed, the black sheep of the family, Hal's younger son, who has been away in the US for ten years: it has all the makings of the return of the prodigal son. Hal picks up his phone, reads the message again and then puts the phone in his pocket. How complicated family relationships can be, especially in this particular case. Fliss is not only his second wife but also his cousin; they married when her husband, Miles, died. Hal and Maria had been divorced for several years by then and he brought their two sons, Jolyon and Edward, to the marriage, while Fliss brought her twin son and daughter. The Chadwicks are a close-knit family. Their home, The Keep, a castellated stone tower in the Devon countryside, has been there for all of them at one time or another, and now Hal and Fliss are the custodians.

Fliss is watching him. 'When you say "coming home",' she says, 'do you mean to England or here?'

Hal grimaces. 'Things haven't gone well in New York. He and Rebecca have split up. Apparently, he's applied for a job in London, but meanwhile he says he'd like to come to see us all. He's been jabbed but he's self-isolating, of course. I'm not sure that he's got anywhere else to go.'

'Well, why not?' says Fliss lightly. 'It will be good to see him.'

Hal pushes the kettle on to the hotplate of the Aga. Since Fliss's niece Lulu and nephew Freddie are both temporarily lodged at The Keep, it would be difficult for her to refuse. And why should she? Ed has always made waves, but it seems unlikely that he will turn up now and cause trouble. Nevertheless, Hal feels a twinge of anxiety. His younger son has a clever way of exposing weaknesses, poking fun, and he hopes that Ed will behave himself.

'Is it to be a long stay?' Fliss is asking, spooning coffee into the cafetiere.

Hal shrugs. 'No idea. You know Ed. Never quite sure what's happening next. I don't suppose he's changed.'

'You don't suppose who's changed?' Freddie

appears in the doorway, a golden Labrador at his heels. 'It's quite chilly up on the hill this morning. Am I in time for coffee?'

'You certainly are.'

As a retired admiral of the fleet, Hal has a lot of respect for Freddie, whose commission as a naval chaplain has just ended. Freddie is debating his future, not certain whether to return to parish ministry or to try a different kind of chaplaincy, and he's been welcomed at The Keep whilst he deliberates.

'Here we are, Honey.' Fliss is filling the dog's water bowl. 'Drink up and you shall have a biscuit.'

Freddie sits down at the refectory table. 'So who hasn't changed?' he repeats.

'Ed's coming for a visit.' It's Fliss who answers him. 'He's moving back and he's applied for a job in London.'

'On his own?' asks Freddie, reaching for his

mug of coffee. 'Thanks, Hal. Has he split with his partner? I've forgotten her name.'

'Rebecca,' Hal reminds him. 'It seems so.'

There's a little silence, except for the sound of Honey lapping water. Nobody speaks but each imagines that the others, too, are thinking about Lulu, whose partner has recently left her and their small son, Oliver, and who, like Freddie, has taken refuge at The Keep.

'Well,' says Freddie cheerfully, 'it looks like it will definitely be a family Christmas, then.'

'Oh, no,' groans Hal. 'Please. Not the C-word. No offence, Freddie.'

Freddie grins at him. 'None taken. A thousand parish priests will be thinking the same thing. Let's just hope we don't have another Covid spike.'

'Don't even think about it,' says Fliss firmly. 'It would be so good to see everyone. The Keep packed, just like in the old days.'

'So just to be clear, Freddie,' says Hal, 'you're not leaving till next year, OK? If it's going to be that sort of Christmas, I shall need your moral support.'

'Aye aye, sir,' says Freddie, grinning at him. 'Suits me.'

'Good man,' says Hal. 'More coffee?'

Fliss watches them. She loves having Freddie and Lulu here. Her sister, Susanna, Freddie and Lulu's mother, was embarrassed when the subject of Freddie's leaving the navy first arose. Freddie would no longer have naval accommodation, and unless he got a place in a parish with a vicarage, he'd have nowhere to live. Fliss was adamant.

'Don't be silly, Sooz,' she said. 'You and Gus haven't got that much space, and Freddie doesn't want to rush into a job just to have a house. That would be crazy, with The Keep just down the lane, and it will be lovely for us to have him. Hal's doing that deaf, grumpy-old-man thing and he's so much better with other people around.'

'You've already got Lulu and Ollie,' Sooz reminded her.

'That's different,' said Fliss. 'It was the perfect solution when the wretched Mark disappeared. And we can all help Lulu with childcare. Anyway, it would be so good for her and Freddie to spend time together. We've hardly seen him for these last five years.'

'It would be great if he could come to you,' Sooz admitted. 'He could rent something, of course, but he's been on his own so much . . .'

'If he'd be happy to be with us we'd love it,' said Fliss. 'The Keep belongs to all of us, remember, not just me and Hal.'

'Thank goodness we're not still in lockdown,'

said Sooz. 'It'll be lovely to have him here for a little while. He's been at sea so much.'

And so it was decided.

Now, Fliss wonders how the dynamic might change with Ed's arrival. She's very fond of his older brother, Jolyon, but Ed was always the tricky one. It's difficult to believe that he's been in the US for ten years, with only a few visits home, and she wonders how he'll like being back. It's strange that these three younger members of the family should all be here at turning points in their lives, and she hopes that she and Hal can help them.

She takes her mug of coffee and sits down in the rocking chair. As usual in moments of stress, she is comforted by familiar things: the long, built-in dresser with its load of pretty china and family bric-a-brac; Honey asleep in the dog basket surrounded by her toys; the warmth from the Aga. Here, more than sixty years ago, she came with Susanna and their brother, Sam, to take refuge with their grandmother after their parents and older brother were murdered by Mau Mau in Kenya. The Keep was a sanctuary for them, the family nourished them, and now Fliss draws strength from it.

CHAPTER TWO

'Ed's coming home,' Freddie says to Lulu. He's been looking for his sister, to share the news with her, and finds her in the kitchen garden rooting up the withered runner beans and taking out the sticks. Summer is over and the harvest gathered, but with its high sheltering stone walls, and warm earthy vegetative scents, this is a good place to be in the autumn sunshine. Lulu's reaction to his news is a kind of puzzled indifference.

'Ed?' she says, resting on her fork, almost as if she's trying to remember who he is. 'We haven't seen him since he came over for his mum's funeral, have we? Has Rebecca been transferred back to the London office?'

'He's coming here. He and Rebecca have split up. Ed's applied for a job in London but he's coming down to stay for a while.'

'Split up?' She looks distressed. 'Poor old Ed. Seems to be running in the family.'

'Perhaps it's Ed that's doing the walking,' says Freddie.

He's a little surprised by his own reaction to the news: a kind of irritation that Ed is coming to disturb the peaceful tenor of things. Yet why should he assume that Ed will do that? Lulu is clearly unmoved by the situation, which makes him feel slightly guilty. Lulu glances at him, sensing his mood.

'Come on,' she says. 'I know he digs at you

for being a priest but that's just Ed. He's harmless really.'

Freddie wants to remind her of Ed's shortcomings – his experimenting with drugs at university, his inability to hold down a job for very long, the way he invested his mother's savings in a dodgy deal and lost the lot – but he resists. He doesn't want to feel like this about Ed and can't quite analyse his reaction. Perhaps it's to do with his own uncertainty at the moment: this lack of knowing where he should go next or what he should do. He seems to have lost his sense of spiritual direction and it worries him.

Lulu is watching him. 'Are Hal and Fliss OK about it? Mum used to say that Ed could be a bit of a problem.'

'I think so.' Freddie pulls himself together and smiles. 'Let's just say that I'm glad I'm in the gatehouse.'

She laughs. 'You can always escape if things get tricky. I wonder how Ollie will like him. Can you bring the bean sticks? I'll need to clean them off or they'll rot. I'll just chuck the vines on the compost.'

She kicks some mud from her boots and they walk back to the greenhouse together.

'It must be nearly lunchtime,' she says, wiping the fork tines with some leaves, then changing into her shoes. 'Shall we go and make a sandwich?'

'Fliss and Hal are meeting friends at the Cott for lunch,' he tells her. 'I thought we might have a little jaunt.'

She smiles at the family expression. 'Where do you have in mind?'

'How about Buckfast?' he asks rather diffidently. 'We could have a bowl of soup in the refectory and then a little wander round the abbey.'

To his relief, she nods. 'That sounds good.'
'We'll take my car,' he says.

As they drive through the narrow lanes between high grassy banks, Lulu thinks about Ed and wonders if the break-up between him and Rebecca has hurt him very much. She still feels the pain of Mark's leaving, unable to forget the things he said to her. He always accused her of being childish. 'Grow up, Lu!' he'd say. 'For Chrissake, you're thirty-five, not fifteen!' Hurtful things, which now she believes were a cover-up for the fact that he was having an affair; to give himself an excuse for betraying her. She knows she's not particularly clever – her elder sister, Alison, is the clever one – and his remarks are still painful to remember.

Through a gateway she glimpses the distant hills of Dartmoor, honey-coloured in the afternoon sunshine. The leaves are beginning to turn, ochre and gold and brown, and the rowan berries glow a bright red. Lulu gives a little sigh, wondering, like Fliss, if Ed will change the dynamic at The Keep. Since Covid closed down the photographic studio in Totnes for a few months she's had very little work and there's something comforting about being at The Keep with Hal and Fliss, and even more so now that Freddie has joined them.

They drive through the abbey's gateway, Freddie parks the car and they walk into the grounds towards the refectory. It's quiet today and they put on their masks, queue at the food bar for soup and rolls, then carry the trays into the refectory to find a table. They chat companionably as they eat: about their father's approaching birthday, Ollie's progress at school. At times like these the pain of betrayal recedes slightly and Lulu can feel at peace.

In the abbey, she lets Freddie precede her as

he walks slowly along the aisle beside the Stations of the Cross, studying each image, and then pauses outside the chapel to look at the amazing east window. She wonders how much he minds that his few attempts at relationships have never worked out. 'Women don't always get on with God,' he said wryly. 'And being at sea for months on end doesn't work either.'

Further on, Freddie pauses by the shelf where the candles, some already lit, stand in rows below a crucifix and she watches as he takes a taper, holds it to a flame and then lights a candle. He replaces the taper and stands quite still, his hands folded, head bowed. Presently he crosses himself, turns to look for her and smiles, and she knows as they walk back together to the car that he too has found a moment of peace.

CHAPTER THREE

Ollie waves goodbye to his friends, climbs on to his bicycle and wobbles away down the lane. He glances back to make certain that Mummy and Uncle Freddie are not too far behind, and then pushes on, singing at the top of his voice. He likes it when Uncle Freddie comes to meet him from school. It's a bit like having Daddy there. It's difficult trying to explain to his friends why his Daddy is never around. Ollie has told them that he's had to go a long way off because of his work, but his friends are a bit puzzled that Ollie never goes to visit him. But now Uncle Freddie is here and he often brings Ollie to school or meets him afterwards.

It's nice being at The Keep, too, because there's no main road so he can ride his bicycle all the way along the lane, to and from school, unless it's pouring with rain. And now a new person is coming to stay. Ed's coming home. Ollie is slightly confused about who Ed is. He knows he's Uncle Jolyon's brother but he's not quite sure why he's coming home from America. Maybe he'll bring really good presents.

Ollie's legs are getting tired. A flock of sheep jostle at a farm gate, their small, sharp hoofs slicing the turf. They watch him inquisitively and then suddenly dash away into the field. He stops cycling, the stabilizers keeping the bike steady, and he looks around.

Mummy waves. 'Nearly there,' she shouts. 'Chocolate brownies for tea,' and he nods and sets off again.

'It's nice, isn't it,' says Lulu as they follow him, 'that we're keeping up tradition. Fourth generation at the village school. D'you remember the Nativity plays?'

Freddie laughs. 'Who could forget them? I remember our dear sister dressed up as Herod and frightening the innkeeper so much he burst into tears.'

'She can still do that to me,' admits Lulu. Unbidden, a jibe of Mark's comes to mind. '"Brilliant sister. Do-no-wrong brother." You're the child of the cul-de-sac who never grows up, Lulu.' It was as if he were quoting something but she didn't ask, just in case it caused another cutting remark.

'Have you thought about school chaplaincy?'

she asks Freddie quickly, more to distract herself than to seek information.

'I've thought about everything,' answers Freddie, rather bitterly. 'These days school chaplains are required to teach, which means I'd have to train first.'

Lulu is silent, wishing she hadn't asked the question. Freddie has always been a private person, rarely sharing his feelings or plans, but she knows that he's finding it hard to adjust and wishes she could help him more. She tries to think of something helpful or positive to say, but everything she thinks of sounds banal or naïve.

Ollie gives a shout – 'Car coming!' – and climbs off his bike, dragging it into the grass verge. Instinctively they both hurry forward, as if ready to protect him, and the moment passes.

Fliss and Susanna are meeting in Bayards Kitchen at the Dartington Cider Press for tea.

'So,' says Susanna, as they sit at the table by the window, 'Ed's coming home. What's all that about?'

Fliss gives a little shake of the head, makes a face. 'Who can tell with Ed? He and Rebecca have split up and he's back from New York. He wants to come and stay for a while. Or until he gets a job.'

'Is Hal OK with that?'

'I think so.' Fliss hesitates. 'You can't always know with Hal. He's never been as close to Ed as he is to Jolyon; Ed was always Maria's boy.'

'Until he invested all her money and lost it,' says Susanna.

'Yes, well,' Fliss sips her tea, 'that certainly wasn't his finest moment, but Hal can't refuse him on those grounds.'

'And not while he's giving shelter to two of my children,' Susanna reminds her. 'I wonder how they'll all get on together. He and Freddie always managed to rub each other up the wrong way when they were younger.'

'Don't,' says Fliss. 'I'm getting too old for family conflict.'

Sooz laughs, glances down the length of the café towards the entrance and gives a groan.

'What?' says Fliss, glancing round. 'Oh, no. Clarissa. That's all we need.'

A tall woman has come in. Her grey hair is bleached an unbecoming blonde and her discontented mouth is bright with lipstick. She catches sight of the sisters and waves enthusiastically.

'Damn,' mutters Fliss, waving back, smiling brightly. 'Get ready for the third degree.'

'Looks like she's on her own,' says Sooz. 'I wonder where Ralph is.'

Fliss snorts. 'Don't ask.'

'Really?' Sooz is amused. 'Is he still . . .?'

'Yes. Ssh.'

Clarissa stops at the counter to order and

then advances up the steps, pulls out a chair, and sits down without waiting to be invited to join them.

'Well, this is good,' she announces, taking off her mask. 'I haven't seen either of you for ages. How's everybody? How's poor Lulu? What a terrible thing. So humiliating, Mark just going off like that. She must be distraught. And poor little Ollie.'

'Oh, we're all coping,' says Fliss quickly. 'How about you? Where's Ralph?'

Clarissa shrugs resentfully. 'He's at one of his meetings. Always some new charity or committee. I tell him if he'd spend half his energy in the garden or the house it would be much more useful. I thought he'd go mad during lockdown.'

The sisters attempt to look sympathetic, suppressing smiles as they swallow their tea.

'It must have been tough for him,' agrees

Sooz, 'not being able to get on with all his good works.'

'He was impossible. Grumpy, sulky. Like a spoilt child.'

Clarissa leans aside as her tea is set in front of her and mutters a thank you. Sooz glances at Fliss, a little nod, and the sisters push back their chairs.

'Got to dash,' Sooz says. 'Sorry, Clarissa. We're meeting Ollie from school.'

'Both of you?' demands Clarissa crossly, disappointed by their defection.

Fliss nods, makes an apologetic face. 'We must make a plan to have a catch-up. Love to Ralph.'

The sisters hurry out, and Fliss bursts out laughing. 'I've never heard adultery called "good works" before,' she says.

'Couldn't resist,' grins Sooz.

'And what's this about meeting Ollie from

school?' Lulu and Freddie went to get him half an hour ago.'

'I know,' says Sooz guiltily. 'But I just couldn't cope with all those toxic questions under the guise of sympathy. Awful woman. I must say I don't blame Ralph. Imagine being in lockdown with Clarissa!'

They laugh as they walk up the slope to the car park.

'Why don't you come back?' asks Fliss. 'You can watch Ollie having his tea.'

'I might do that,' says Sooz. 'Gus won't be back from Exeter yet.'

Fliss raises her eyebrows. '"Good works"?'

Sooz laughs. 'He should be so lucky! He's gone to Exeter to buy a new laptop.'

'That's what he told you,' says Fliss. 'But can we trust him?'

'Gus is much too lazy,' grins Sooz. 'Choir rehearsal is quite enough. Good works would completely finish him off. See you in a minute.'

They climb into their respective cars and drive away towards The Keep.

Clarissa watches them go and then turns to stare out of the window. She isn't aware of the sparkle of the little stream below, or the arrow-flash of the dipper's flight: all her thoughts are inward. She's frustrated by the sisters' departure. She's worked hard at being best friends with them, especially Fliss: Lady Chadwick. She likes to brag about them to her friends – Admiral Sir Hal has a certain ring to it – but somehow Fliss manages to evade a real closeness. Clarissa suspects that they know that Ralph likes to play the field. He's always had an eye for the ladies, but she's never been able to catch him out. There are always good reasons for his absences, his trips away. She's even suspected his sister-in-law, Lizzie, but Ralph has explanations for his visits to her, especially since his brother died and he's one of the executors of his brother's will.

Clarissa sits back in her chair, sips her tea and looks around her. It would be very satisfying to play Ralph at his own game but she's never been good at the lightness of touch required for a flirtation. She tried it once with Hal but he was humiliatingly kind, bantering, smiling, as if he were humouring a child in a game, and she felt embarrassed and frustrated. As she sits, contemplating the sweetness of revenge, an odd thing happens. A man has come into the coffee shop with a woman and now they sit opposite each other, the woman on the banquette against the wall, and the man facing her. The man is Gus, Susanna's husband.

They immediately embark on an animated conversation while Clarissa watches them, intrigued. It seems so odd that Gus should arrive so quickly after Susanna's departure, and that he should be so taken up with this woman, who looks rather younger and is very pretty. She is talking now, gesticulating, and Gus watches her, nodding encouragingly.

Clarissa feels elated. She remembers how the sisters hurried away from her, how they have resisted any real closeness, and now she sees an opportunity for a different kind of revenge. Not to do with Ralph but simply to pay off a few scores with the Chadwicks.

She pushes back her chair, stands up and, picking up her bag, goes down the few steps so that she is directly behind Gus's chair.

'Hi, Gus,' she says, touching him lightly on the shoulder.

He turns quickly, his expression changing

almost comically to dismay at the sight of her, and she hurries away before he can speak. At the door she glances back and is delighted to see him still looking after her with the anxious expression still on his face.

CHAPTER FOUR

Ed drives beneath the archway of the gate-house, stops the car, and sits for a moment in the courtyard, staring up at the three-storey, castellated tower. There have been Chadwicks at The Keep for nearly two hundred years. An ancestor, returning from the Far East with a considerable fortune, purchased the ruined hill fort between the moors and the sea, and rebuilt it with the stones lying about the site. The wings, two storeys high and set back on each side of the house, were later additions, along with the courtyard with its high stone walls and gatehouse. Old-fashioned roses and wisteria climb the courtyard walls and the newer wings, but the austere grey tower itself remains unadorned.

Ed sits looking around and smiles a little. Nothing has changed. He feels rather like the prodigal son returning home with very little to show for his absence.

Even as he thinks it, his father and Freddie appear around the side of the house with a golden Labrador at their heels. They are laughing and talking together, and his sense of inadequacy is suddenly sharp. They see him and come towards him and he climbs quickly out of the car, feeling at less of a disadvantage if he's standing. His father shakes his hand, Freddie smiles at him, and Ed bends to stroke the dog, grateful for the distraction. As they stand, talking about his journey, exchanging greetings, Fliss comes out and calls a welcome to him. He goes to greet her and she holds out her arms to him, hugging him, and he's oddly touched and grateful for this sign of affection.

'It's good to see you, Ed,' she says. 'Come on in. We'll sort out your luggage later.'

He follows her into the garden room, where his father and Freddie kick off their boots and give the dog a quick rub down with a rather muddy towel.

'Coffee,' Fliss is saying, going through to the kitchen. 'Would you like some, Ed? Or are you a tea man?'

He doesn't want to feel like a stranger, a guest, so he sits down at the long refectory table without waiting to be asked, smiling at them all, reminding himself that Freddie also has no job and no home at the moment, which brings a small measure of comfort to Ed in his vulnerable state.

'Definitely coffee,' he says. 'Thanks, Fliss.'

He looks around him at the patchwork curtains and matching cushions, the bright rugs on the old flagstones, the dog basket beside the Aga. It's a familiar and comforting scene. But before he can speak, voices are heard in the passage, the door is flung open and a small boy rushes in. He stops suddenly, staring around until he sees Ed sitting at the table.

'Are you Ed?' he demands. 'Is that your car outside?'

'Yes, it is,' says Ed, smiling. 'Do you have a problem with that?'

'No! It's awesome,' he replies solemnly, and everyone laughs. 'Can we go for a ride in it?'

'Well,' begins Ed cautiously, wondering how it might be managed in his two-seater. 'We'll have to see about that.'

'Mummy says you've come all the way from America. Have you brought me a present?'

There's a general protest from all the adults, and Lulu, arriving in time to hear it, is clearly embarrassed.

'Ollie,' she cries, 'that's very rude. Sorry, Ed,' she adds. 'Hi. It's great to see you again. It's been much too long. This is Ollie.'

'It's great to see you, too,' he says, feeling suddenly at ease. 'And no, I haven't brought a present for you, Ollie, because I wasn't sure what you might like so I thought we might go shopping together and you could choose. What d'you think?'

'Awesome!' cries Ollie again.

Ed sees his father's nod of approval, Freddie's amused but slightly quizzical glance, Lulu's smile of pleasure, and he relaxes in his chair and smiles his thanks to Fliss as she pours his coffee.

Round one to the prodigal son, he thinks.

*

Ed's return home is going well. Freddie takes his coffee and retires to the window seat to watch his family. Ollie is unwittingly helping the reunion along. His questions, his eagerness to show this new friend his toys, cover the awkwardness that might have accompanied Ed's explanations and reasons for his return. As it is, Hal and Fliss smile at Ollie's excitement whilst Lulu tries to contain his exuberance. Because it's a Saturday there is plenty of the day left for Ollie to get to know Ed, and presently he agrees to go upstairs to see Ollie's train set whilst Fliss and Hal sort out lunch.

As Ed pushes back his chair he glances across at Freddie, and raises his eyebrows as if wondering if he's going to accompany them, but Freddie gives a little shake of the head. The very slight shrugging of Ed's shoulders makes Freddie feel as if he's being a bit of a spoilsport but he remains where he is, watching them go,

Ollie chattering at the top of his voice. Then Fliss pushes back her chair and Hal watches her, an odd expression on his face. Freddie suspects that they might want to talk about Ed and decides to give them some privacy. He stands up, rinses his mug out and smiles at them.

'Got a few things to do,' he says. 'See you later. Unless I can do anything to help . . .?'

'No, it's all simple stuff,' says Fliss. 'Give us about half an hour.'

Freddie nods and heads back outside, crossing the courtyard and going into the gatehouse. It's been renovated since Fox, the gardener and handyman, lived here back in the fifties, and Freddie goes into a big room that is now both study and sitting room, with a wood-burner in the stone fireplace and bookshelves lining one whole wall. When he moved in, Fliss brought over a box of books that belonged to his great-uncle Theo, also a priest and naval chaplain, and Freddie enjoys looking through them, hoping for inspiration in his own situation.

Now Freddie stands for a moment, hands in his pockets, head bent. He is rather surprised by his feelings: a slight sense of resentment that Ollie should so quickly take to Ed, that Lulu welcomed him with so much affection. He knows that he is being childish and he mutters an imprecation under his breath. His state of mind worries him: his indecision, his disaffection with his ministry. He has no sense of direction.

He sits at the round oak table and thinks, as he so often does in these moments, of his old friend and mentor, Sister Emily, at the Retreat House, Chi-Meur, in north Cornwall. During the worst of the Covid pandemic, Chi-Meur was closed, but now it's opened its doors again and Freddie wonders if he should have a sabbatical there, a few weeks to help him to focus.

He thinks again about Ed, who is able to irritate him so easily, and he wonders why it should be so. Surely his vocation should enable him to take this sort of thing in his stride but, since they were children, Ed's always been able to get under his skin. Freddie feels guilty that he's pleased that Ed is also without a home or a job or a partner, and is angry with himself for being so mean-spirited. He stands up, ducking to avoid the great central beam, and goes to the bookshelf. Not really studying the titles, he takes down a book and looks at it. *The Impact of God: Soundings from St John of the Cross* – one of Theo's books. He opens it at random and sees the translation of the prayer of a Soul in Love.

Who can free himself from his meanness and
    limitations,
if you do not lift himself to yourself, my God,
    in purity of love?

How will a person
brought to birth and nurtured in a world of
    small horizons,
rise up to you, Lord,
if *you* do not raise him by the hand which
    made him?
You will not take from me, my God,
what you once gave me
in your only son, Jesus Christ,
in whom you gave me all I desire;
so I shall rejoice:
you will not delay, if I do not fail to hope.

Freddie takes the book and sits down again at the table: 'meanness and limitations' seem particularly apt just at the moment. He begins to read.

When Fliss knocks at the door, he leaps up, cracks his head on the beam and lets out a howl of frustration.

'Are you OK?' she asks, putting her head round the door.

'Yes,' he answers quickly. 'Yes, of course. Sorry, I got absorbed in something. Is it lunchtime?'

They go out together and she links her arm in his as they cross the courtyard. Her affection soothes but also slightly irritates him because he suspects that there is an element of pity in it. He wants to tell her he's fine, that he's a big boy now, that he can cope with Ed, but she forestalls him.

'I'm really glad you're here,' she tells him. 'Hal always finds Ed a bit tricky. He was always so much Maria's boy. But it's much easier with other people around.'

She squeezes his arm and lets it go, and, slightly taken aback, confused but pleased, he follows her into the house.

CHAPTER FIVE

Ed climbs into his car, drives out of the stable yard, around the courtyard and away down the lane. Lulu and Ollie have set off for school, Fliss and Hal are discussing gardening and taking Honey for a walk, and Freddie has not yet appeared from the gatehouse. Ed is feeling the need to be alone, to escape for a while from this whole new experience of family life. He's gratified by the reception he's been given – especially by small Ollie – but slightly taken off balance by it. He's not used to small children or living in a large family unit and he wants some space.

He drives away, not certain where he's going but remembering that Totnes is the nearest town. Lulu drove him in to show him the photographic studio huddling beneath the castle walls, explaining how, since Covid, she's been running it on her own, and then they wandered round the Friday market amongst the colourful stalls, paused to listen to the buskers, and had coffee in a coffee shop in the medieval high street.

'Bit of a change from New York,' he said, smiling at her across the table.

'I can imagine,' she answered. 'But I love it. Alison keeps telling me I should get out, make a change, but ... I don't know. It's just my place, I guess.'

He watched her for a moment, sensing a defensiveness. 'And Alison is your sister?

That's right, isn't it? Sorry, there's so many of us I get a bit confused.'

She nodded. 'Big sister. Freddie is eldest, Alison next, then me. Littlest, least and last.'

'And what does Alison do?'

'She's a solicitor in Bristol, married to a doctor. She was always the clever one.'

Ed gave a little shrug. 'I think it's rather cool to have your own photographic studio and to have survived through the pandemic and still be up and running. Sounds like fun.'

'It is, actually. Lots of people are doing Airbnb now, especially around here, and they need photos and videos so it's going quite well. And Dad's really pleased that he can retire and I'm carrying it on.'

As Ed drives into Totnes he thinks about that defensiveness, the 'littlest, least and last', and sympathizes. His is a different situation but he feels a little bit like that about his older brother,

Jolyon: television presenter, happily married, two children, beloved at The Keep. Neither he nor Lulu have talked about their personal lives but there is a kind of unspoken empathy between them, a mutual understanding. Ed is well aware of how much Ollie's presence has helped to ease his way back to his family. Ollie is delighted to have a new cousin, back from America with a sports car and a good instinct for the right kinds of books and toys, and Ed knows he's gaining brownie points. And he's actually enjoying this new experience. He's aware of the family's efforts not to talk about Rebecca, to refrain from asking questions, and he's grateful. It's so difficult maintaining the pretence, keeping his secrets. On the other hand, it's easy being the fun cousin who has no responsibility.

He wonders if Freddie's nose has been put slightly out of joint by Ollie's affection but he isn't showing it. Ed still feels the instinct to tease, to poke and prod, but Freddie isn't rising to Ed's baiting. He'd like to question Freddie about what he plans to do next, what he's thinking and feeling about being without a job, but he's afraid that Freddie might ask him the same question. How good it would be to make a clean breast of things. Perhaps it was foolish of him to believe that he could do it.

Ed parks where Lulu showed him, nearly opposite the photographic studio. He buys a ticket, locks the car and heads off into the town.

Leaving Fliss in the garden room, putting on her boots ready for a session in the kitchen garden, Hal walks out through the stable yard towards the hill, climbing the well-worn paths, crisscrossed with sheep tracks. Mist curls through the valley below, revealing ghostly shapes – slowly moving cattle, feathery tree tops – but here, higher up, the sun is shining. The tors of the moor are visible in the distance, sketched along the horizon, rocks piled by a giant's hand above the bracken-covered slopes. Familiar though it is to Hal, this scene always brings delight: the patchwork of small neat fields and villages, the silvery gleam of river water.

Two rooks, disturbed in their feeding by Honey, flap up, croaking raucously as they go, and Hal walks on, thinking about his family. His sense of responsibility encompasses them all: Lulu trying to plan a new life without Mark, which needs to work for her and Ollie; Freddie, who seems to have lost his way since leaving the navy; Ed, who never lets anyone get too close, who insists that he has several irons in the fire, that this is just a breathing space. Hal knows that all three of them are adults who need to sort out their own lives, but he and Fliss can't help but worry about them, to want what is best – whatever that might be – for them. The pandemic has changed so much, destroyed so much, but he and Fliss are determined that the family must pull together now to get them all back on track.

He pauses to look back down the hill. Thank God for The Keep, he thinks, that small stone fortress, protecting them all. The real problem is that he feels helpless, unable to direct or advise, unsure what is best for these three who are no longer children yet seem so vulnerable.

'If we can just go with it,' Fliss said, 'we can make it a happy time. It's lovely to have them here. Really great to have the house busy, used. *Carpe diem*, and all that. I love it that Ollie is in the nursery where we were when we came back from Kenya. OK, so I don't love the reasons why he and Lulu are here, but we can try to turn it round and make it positive. And dear old

Freddie. I can't blame women for not liking the idea of those long separations, but maybe now he can find somewhere to settle. And Ed . . .'

She paused then, not quite knowing what to say about Ed. Her twins, Bess and Jamie, have fulfilled, happy lives, but Hal knows that she's just as concerned about Ed as she is for her niece and nephew, and he's grateful to her. Ed is such a difficult person to get close to; something about him makes it impossible to question him, to find out about his circumstances. He evades any kind of probing about his work, except that he's in IT, and he seems quite calm about finding another job – if not the one he's applied for in London, then some other. Hal hears his phone ping and he takes it out of his pocket. It's a message from Fliss.

Sooz has offered to bring lunch over.

Gus is supplying the wine. Are you happy with that? x

Hal smiles. This is their way of sharing and he is touched by it. He taps out an answer.

Definitely. x

He whistles to Honey and they start the descent. Hal feels calm again: ready to face the day. And what a day it is: late autumn sunshine, a glint of gold on the trees, the flick and flitter of a flock of finches in the furze. It's been strange to see the sky free of aeroplanes: no chalky trails sketched across the blue board of the sky, only a buzzard hovering high above him. Fliss is right: *Carpe diem.*

In the kitchen garden, Fliss pauses from her task of digging in compost. The soil is still warm from the summer and she's planning ahead for next year. She loves it here. Presently she will pick the last of the red and yellow Sunset apples from the cordon trees that grow on the high walls, and there is some kale, too, looking like quill pens, which she will harvest.

As she plans for next spring she's thinking about Ed and Lulu and Freddie: wondering what will happen, how their lives will unfold. The Covid restrictions have eased, much more is open to them now, but there are still difficulties. Lulu talks of getting a flat in Totnes, but there is very little rental accommodation available and it seems foolish to go to the trouble and expense of finding somewhere whilst there is so much room here. But Fliss can see that Lulu might like to have more privacy, the opportunity to meet someone new. It's good to see her getting along so well with Ed, though occasionally Fliss wonders if Freddie is feeling slightly sidelined. Ollie clearly loves his new cousin. It's Ed who is now chosen to read the bedtime story, to go on the school run. Freddie seems perfectly fine with it, but Fliss knows that her nephew doesn't show his feelings readily. Certainly Ed has introduced a new, lighter spirit into their little circle although he and Freddie still maintain the wariness that has always coloured their relationship. It's clear that Ed's sharp witticisms about the Church still irritate Freddie, who finds it difficult to laugh them off. Sometimes she leaps to his defence, which doesn't really help: it embarrasses Freddie and amuses Ed.

Why do relationships have to be so complicated, wonders Fliss, as she puts the fork in the wheelbarrow and pushes it back to the greenhouse. She worries about Lulu, too. Fliss sees that Mark has damaged Lulu's confidence, lowered her self-esteem, and she wonders how it can be restored. Ed's easy-going, cheerful approach to life seems to appeal to Lulu, but Fliss knows that Ed also has his problems. He's evasive about what his future plans are, what jobs he's applying for – the job he was after in London seems not to have come to anything – and what his financial situation is. He's simply staying for just a few weeks, so he doesn't contribute as Freddie and Lulu do, but he's very generous, buying delicious treats, bottles of wine, presents for Ollie.

As she puts the fork away, leans the wheelbarrow against the wall, Fliss is slightly relieved that Ed has messaged to say that he won't be back for lunch. He's decided to explore Totnes and have a walk along the river. She wonders if he plans to meet up with Lulu, who is working at the studio. Freddie has gone to Exeter to meet an old friend so it will be just the four of them, which will be good. Susanna and Gus know the situation and are very tactful. Nevertheless, conversation can sometimes be tricky when it comes to discussing any plans for the future with their young, and Fliss is looking forward to a relaxed lunch.

Whilst she packs two baskets with pâté, cheese, sourdough bread and home-made soup, Susanna is thinking about Gus. He's been just a tad odd recently: preoccupied, jumpy. If it were anyone but Gus she might be a bit suspicious – especially since Clarissa told her that she saw him in Bayards Kitchen with a woman. She dropped it casually into the conversation but there was a kind of awful glee about her manner, a watchfulness in her small brown eyes, that made Susanna feel quite cross.

'Might be anyone,' she answered Clarissa indifferently. 'One of the choir members. Or a client. He's mostly retired, but he still helps Lulu out now and again.'

Clarissa shrugged, made some laughing

remark, but the little seed had lodged and grown. It's unlike Gus to be edgy and she can't think of any good reason for it. At one point she even repeated Clarissa's conversation and watched for his response. Was that a flicker of anxiety in his eyes? But he laughed it off.

'What a poisonous cow that woman is,' he said lightly. 'Poor old Ralph. How does he bear it now that he's retired?'

Susanna found that it was impossible to question him further – it seemed to demean their relationship – but it was clear that there was something on his mind. Now he appears in the kitchen carrying a bottle of wine in each hand, holding them out so that she can see the label.

'Sharpham's Dart Valley Reserve,' he says. 'I thought the occasion demanded something special.'

He looks happy, at ease, and she relaxes.

'It'll be good to see them on their own,' she says. 'There are so many pitfalls at the moment. I wish Freddie could find a parish. I worry about him.'

Gus puts the wine into the baskets and folds his arms around her.

'I know you do,' he says. 'But something will turn up. He needs to want to do the job or he won't be happy.'

She holds him tightly. 'I know that really. But he's such a funny old thing. I feel I can't reach him at the moment.'

He kisses the top of her head, gives her another hug. 'I feel the same, but it will come right. I know it.'

She smiles at him. This is the old Gus, her rock. How foolish to be even momentarily alarmed by Clarissa's poison.

'Sorry,' she says. 'Just having a wobble. OK. Let's get this show on the road.'

CHAPTER SIX

There's a letter waiting for Freddie when he comes into the kitchen the following morning.

'A real letter,' says Ed, making big eyes. 'Actual handwriting on the envelope and everything.'

Freddie takes the letter from Fliss, pretending to ignore Ed whilst overcoming a desire to smack him. He looks at the handwriting and then puts the letter in the back pocket of his jeans. He wonders why he finds Ed's teasing so difficult to cope with and wishes he could be lighter spirited, ready to joke and laugh.

'Hal's taken Honey up on the hill,' Fliss says, clearly aware of the tension. 'Lulu's taken Ollie to school and is going on to the studio. I'm going into Totnes. Very welcome to come with me.'

She glances from one to the other and Freddie suddenly decides that he'd like to do that. To escape from his anxieties and have some company. He'll read his letter later.

'That would be great,' he says. 'Thanks.'

He can see that Ed is hesitating – maybe it's one of those 'Two's company, three is none' moments – then he shakes his head.

'I'll give it a miss,' he says, and Freddie feels a sense of relief.

'I'll grab a jacket,' he says to Fliss, 'and see you out there.'

He glances at Ed as he goes out but Ed is

staring at a message that's just come in on his phone and doesn't notice.

'Do you need to do any shopping?' asks Fliss, as she locks the car. 'I'm going to Halls and the farm shop but we can meet in the Terrace afterwards for coffee.'

'No, I'm fine,' he answers. 'I might get a newspaper. See you later.'

He likes the Terrace Coffee Shop, built on the ruins of the old priory, set above the passageway leading to the high street, with its whitewashed walls and the big stone fireplace. The owners, Rob and Andy, always give them a warm welcome and it's a peaceful place to sit by the windows in the sunshine with the cyclamen in the window boxes. Rob brings him a cappuccino and Freddie takes the letter from his back pocket and settles down to read it. He'd recognized the writing, of course, when

Ed joked about it, but had no intention of telling him that it was from Sister Emily at Chi-Meur, knowing that it would probably raise more amusement, more humorous comments. Now in her eighties, Sister Emily prefers the art of letter writing to emails, and Freddie is glad. It's good to have her letters, to be able to carry them about and reread them. She is his mentor. She keeps him in touch with the news of the retreat house. They now have conferences and weddings, as well as retreats, and his old friend Janna is still looking after the few remaining sisters. Sister Emily knows of his dilemma, that he is in the desert, and her love and support are very special to him. The letter opens with the usual greeting:

Freddie beloved,

I have been holding you in prayer each day at Morning Prayer and again in the silence before Compline. Try not to feel too despairing about your resentment towards your cousin when he teases you. Even Christ lost his temper in the temple.

And Ed's teasing is probably masking some inadequacy of his own. Perhaps you could help him. You ask for something to read and I wonder if you might find Michael Mayne's 'Learning to Dance' as uplifting as I do. There's a chapter for each month of the year and I'm finding October particularly life-affirming. This month is the 'Dance of Love'. There's a quote from St John of the Cross. 'When the evening of this life comes, we shall be judged on love.' Very thought-provoking.

St John of the Cross. Ed pauses, folding the letter, remembering what he had been read-ing earlier. 'Who can free himself from his meanness and limitations . . .' But how could he possibly help Ed, even if he wanted to, which just at the moment he doesn't?

The café door opens and there is Fliss. Rob and Andy are welcoming her, making her coffee, and Freddie gives an inward sigh of relief; glad to be distracted.

'I've cheated,' says Fliss, sitting down, 'and bought pasties for lunch. Hal loves Halls' pasties.'

'Sounds good to me,' answers Freddie. 'So what are we going to do about his birthday? Have you got a plan . . .?'

When they get home Hal is nowhere to be seen but Ed is sitting at the kitchen table, drinking coffee with Honey in attendance. He has an odd expression, preoccupied, wary.

'Hi,' he says. 'So was it fun?'

His tone manages to imply that fun is an unlikely possibility with your aunt in a small market town, but that Freddie might be desperate enough to find it so.

'It depends how you define fun,' answers Freddie equably, helping Fliss unpack the bags. 'I enjoyed it.'

The old antagonism is back and Freddie feels the usual mix of guilt and irritation. He remembers that when they left, Ed was staring at a message on his phone.

'How about you?' he asks. 'Been messaging your friends?'

The look Ed gives him is quick, suspicious, almost guilty, and Freddie is taken aback. He responds to it instinctively, thinking of Sister Emily's letter.

'Fliss has bought pasties for lunch,' he says casually, 'so that's easy. How about we take Honey out on the hill to get our appetites up?'

Ed is still looking at him with that odd expression and now he gives a kind of facial shrug, lifting his eyebrows, pulling down the corners of his mouth.

'Why not?' he says almost with indifference.

'Great,' says Freddie. 'I'll go and change my shoes.'

When he gets into the gatehouse he pauses for a moment, surprised at himself. He takes Sister Emily's letter from his pocket and drops it on the table, then notices that there are a couple more lines on the back of the sheet. He picks it up again and reads her words.

PS. This book might not be for you, Freddie beloved, and don't worry if it isn't. But who knows? Maybe it's time you learned to dance.

He stares at the words for a moment, then he tucks the letter in between the leaves of a book, changes his shoes, and goes back out to find Ed and Honey.

Fliss watches them go with a mix of surprise and pleasure. It would be such a relief if these two could find an amicable way forward, rather than the bantering and bickering that is never very far away in their relationship. It's odd that she's more worried about Ed than she is about Freddie. Freddie seems to have lost his sense of direction but there's something about Ed, a continual brightness, the need to keep everyone laughing, that she suspects is a veneer to hide something. But what? She and Hal have talked about it but never come to a conclusion. Ed doesn't seem too heartbroken about the break-up with Rebecca, and he doesn't seem to be short of money.

'I'm not even sure what it is he does,' Hal said. 'I find the IT stuff very confusing. He baffles me with science. I'm just worried that he's done something foolish, like when he lost Maria's investments, and he's just keeping his head down.'

'You mean he's hiding from creditors?' Fliss was momentarily alarmed but instinct told her that this is not the reason for Ed's visit.

Hal shook his head. 'I don't really think so, but that's the trouble with Ed. You just never quite know. There's an instability.'

Now, as she puts away the shopping, Fliss thinks about that remark. It's true; all that glitter and gleam, smoke and mirrors, but who is the real Ed? She hates the idea that he can't confide in them but there's little she can do: she's not his mother. At least she can offer him refuge. Maybe Freddie can win his confidence, and she wonders what they're talking about, out there on the hill.

*

Following Hal into Bayards Kitchen, Susanna sees Clarissa too late to beat a retreat. She waves enthusiastically, indicating the spare chairs, and Susanna waves back, cursing under her breath.

'At least she's got Ralph with her,' says Hal, as they order their coffee at the counter. 'Want a croissant?'

'Tempting,' she answers, 'but I shall resist. How about you?'

He shakes his head. 'Fliss said she might get pasties for lunch. Come on. Once more unto the breach and all that.'

'How nice to see you,' cries Clarissa brightly as they sit down. 'But odd to see you together without Gus or Fliss.'

She glances inquisitively between them as if demanding an explanation.

'I know,' Hal smiles blandly at her. 'But there we are. You've found us out at last. We shall just have to beg you to keep it to yourselves.'

Susanna wants to laugh out loud at Clarissa's expression, but manages not to simply because Ralph looks so uncomfortable.

'How are you?' he asks.

'You must be so busy,' Clarissa says before they can answer. 'I was saying to Ralph that it must be so odd having your adult children living with you again. I do admire you. I can't see Selina wanting to come back to live with us.'

There's an awkward little silence whilst the words 'And I can quite imagine why!' hang unspoken in the air.

'Fliss and I are really enjoying it,' answers Hal calmly. 'You rarely get the privilege of having young people around when you get to our ages. We're making the most of it.'

Clarissa is silenced and the coffee arrives, so there's a moment before any of them speak again.

'So how are you doing, Ralph?' asks Susanna,

managing to refrain from using the words 'good works'. 'I saw something about you in the paper raising funds for Totnes Caring. Well done.'

He smiles at her. 'Thank you, but it's not just me. They're a great team.'

'It certainly takes up a lot of his time,' says Clarissa tartly, and there's another awkward silence.

'And how's Gus?' she asks then, with a kind of concerned sympathy, and Susanna's heart sinks, hoping she's not going to comment again on seeing him with a young woman.

'Gus is another busy fellow,' replies Hal before she can speak. 'It's great that he can be singing again. Thank goodness we can all get out and about after lockdown. Let's hope we don't get another spike this winter.'

Covid dominates the conversation for a moment and then Ralph says that they should be moving. Clarissa looks disappointed, but they've finished their coffee and Ralph is already standing up, collecting coats and bags.

'There seemed to be a certain sense of tension around all that,' observes Hal, sipping his coffee. 'Is there something I should know?'

Susanna fiddles with the biscuit in her saucer, notices that the music in the background is '50 Ways to Leave Your Lover' and gives a little snort of exasperation.

'She saw Gus in here with a young woman and now she's hinting that he might be playing around.'

'And is he?' asks Hal, grinning. 'Why can't I imagine Gus playing around?'

'Thanks for that,' she says. 'I did actually mention what Clarissa said but he was almost indifferent. Just said how poisonous she is.'

'And?' Hal is watching her, waiting.

'I expect it was a choir member, but the odd thing was that it was an afternoon when he said he was going to Exeter.'

'So how did he explain that?'

'He didn't. I didn't question him. It was too . . . I don't know . . . well, degrading. Do you know what I mean?'

'Yes, I think so,' says Hal after a moment. 'After all these years it's too ludicrous to think about.'

'Yes,' she says gratefully. 'It would undermine both of us.' She gives a little shiver. 'The trouble is that Clarissa's already sown a nasty seed of suspicion. And I have to admit that Gus is being just a little bit odd.'

'How d'you mean?'

'Well, nothing I could really put my finger on, but a bit distracted. Keeping his phone under strict control.' She shrugs. 'I'm probably being paranoid, but that's what I mean. That poisonous cow has sown a little seed of doubt and I can't quite uproot it.'

Hal is silent for a moment, leaning back, glancing around him.

'Does Fliss know?'

'No,' Susanna answers quickly. 'And I don't really want her to. Sorry, Hal. Not fair to tell you then ask you to keep it to yourself. Gosh, I hate this.'

'OK,' he says calmly. 'That's not a problem. I don't believe it for a moment, but mightn't it be better to be absolutely open with Gus? He'll understand.'

'I know, and I do think about it, but then it's so humiliating to actually ask the question.'

'Yes, I get that. Where is he, by the way?'

'He's at home. I just dashed out to get a birthday card for someone, and there you were buying some wine. I felt we deserved coffee.'

'We did.' He smiles at her. 'How about both

of you coming over for supper? Ed's making one of his famous Thai green curries.'

'That sounds good,' she answers. For some silly reason she feels a bit weepy. She hates feeling like this about Gus and it would be good to have a real family evening. 'Yes,' she says. 'It's a date.'

CHAPTER SEVEN

November

It's Hal who lights the first fire of the year in the hall. He's already built a wigwam of kindling on the granite hearthstone, tucking a firelighter deep within it, and carefully placing twigs and small logs on the flames as they take hold. There's a large log basket in its own alcove within the deep recess of the fireplace and it's his job to make certain that it's kept piled high with dry logs throughout the winter.

Two high-backed sofas, heaped with cushions, face each other across the long, low oak
table and at the end of it a deep comfortable
armchair stands opposite the fireplace. It's a
room within a room, a warm cosy space within
the vaster, draughty spaces of the hall. Hal sits
on the little stool beside the alcove, watching
the flames take hold, as they creep along the
small twigs, licking around the smaller logs.

He wishes that Susanna had never told him
about her suspicions regarding Gus. Keeping it
from Fliss has been much more difficult than he
anticipated and once or twice she's asked if he
has something on his mind. Luckily there's
always Ed to fall back on, anxieties about his
future and so on, but nevertheless he's not
happy with the deception. His birthday supper
went well, everyone cheerful, and Gus certainly didn't look like a man with a guilty secret.
In fact, it's Ed who is behaving more like that:

giving a little start if his phone buzzes, looking preoccupied, and not quite so ready to tease Freddie. And Freddie seems to have no direction, no focus.

Hal sighs and leans forward to place another log on the fire, which is now blazing up in a very satisfactory way. It's been a warm November, glorious autumn colours, bronze and yellow and red, but now Storm Arwen has swept in and most of the trees stand bare and exposed. Fliss and Freddie are sweeping up leaves, a job they both enjoy, and Honey is with them, Lulu is fetching Ollie from school and they will all be coming in to tea. Hal places a few more logs on the fire, wonders where Ed is, and goes into the kitchen to fill the kettle.

Ed is standing at his bedroom window, staring across the meadow to the line of trees at the hedge's boundary. Ollie's bedroom is directly above his, in the nursery, and Ed looks at the trees, trying to make out the faces and shapes that Ollie sees. It's a still, quiet afternoon and as he stares intently he can begin to see, although now that the leaves are nearly gone it's not so easy to make out the faces amongst the branches. There's a big twiggy profile – jutting nose, big chin – and he sees an ivy-covered tree that looks as if it is dancing, arms flung up high.

His phone rings. Ed stares at the caller's number but makes no attempt to answer it. After it's stopped ringing a message pings in.

Come on, Ed. Please answer. I can see you're ghosting me so stop this and get in touch. Nick's told me you are back but no one seems to know where you are. I know there are all sorts of problems but can't we just work it out? I've missed you. I know you've got family in the West Country so maybe I can track you down. Love you. x

Ed turns away from the window, filled with panic. 'Panic and emptiness' – E. M. Forster's words seem to sum up Ed's life just now and he feels a ridiculous desire to burst into tears. He needs courage, strength, but from where shall he find them? His life has been such a mess. He stares at the message and wonders if it is possible to wipe the slate clean and start again. Is it possible? Where could he start? The mere idea makes him shiver. He hears voices, Ollie calling out his name, and, putting his phone in his pocket, Ed goes down to meet him.

As soon as Freddie comes into the kitchen from the garden room he can see that all is not well with Lulu. Hal has already begun to organize the tea tray and though he is talking to Lulu, Freddie can see that she's not really concentrating. There's a little frown between her brows and she's clearly distracted. Hal is taking the tray, calling some instruction about making the tea over his shoulder, but she doesn't seem to be listening.

'Everything OK?' Freddie asks lightly. 'I'll make some tea, shall I?'

She looks at him, glances quickly around. 'I've had an email from Mark,' she says. 'He wants to come and see Ollie. He's even asking if he can stay. I mean, seriously? We hardly ever hear from him, it's been two years, but suddenly it's like nothing ever happened.'

'Have you answered the email?'

'No, of course not. I was just leaving the studio when it came in. It's just knocked me off balance.'

'Well, that's reasonable,' Freddie says calmly. 'Don't panic about this. We'll sort something out. You're in control here.'

'It's not that I don't want him to see Ollie, it's just that he's been so casual about it.'

Freddie tries to think how she can deal with this, but before he can speak Fliss comes in, pulling a jersey on.

'It's very chilly,' she says. 'I'm glad Hal has lit the fire. Are you coming?'

'Yes, of course,' answers Freddie. 'We're making tea. Well, coffee for Ed, of course.'

'I'll see what Hal's taken through,' she says, and goes out.

'Let's talk about this later,' Freddie says. 'I imagine you won't be telling Hal and Fliss just yet?'

'God no!' says Lulu. 'I need time to process it. But I simply can't have him here. I mean, he just walked out. Told me he'd been having this affair with Anneke for months and that he was going back to the Netherlands with her. Goodbye and thanks for all the fish.'

She looks angry, hurt, and turns quickly away as Ollie comes running in.

'Granny's got some good games,' he shouts. 'Come and see, Mummy.'

'I'm coming,' she answers. 'I'll be right there. Just finding that cake you like. Go and tell Granny I'm just coming.'

He disappears again and Freddie puts his arm round Lulu's shoulder and gives her a quick hug.

'Let's talk later when Ollie's in bed. But try not to panic. We're all here.'

She gives a huge sigh and he feels her relax.

'Sorry,' she says. 'I'm being a bit crazy. You're right. What can he do?'

'Good,' he says. 'Don't worry. We'll set Ed on him. That'll show him.'

She gives a little smile. 'Thanks, Freddie. I'm OK now. Can you make Ed's coffee and I'll do the tea?'

When they come into the hall Ollie is sitting on a stool at the end of the long, low table, with Ed and Fliss sitting on each side on the sofas and they are playing a very noisy game of snap. They barely glance up, and Lulu is pleased to sit at the other end of the sofa beside the fire with Honey, watching Hal dealing with the plates and mugs.

She hadn't expected to be so affected by Mark's email. All the pain and resentment has come flooding back, along with a fear that this life that she has made with Ollie and her family might be disrupted. Of course, it would be good if Mark and Ollie could establish a closer relationship, but Ollie was only three when Mark left and, with Covid restrictions, visiting has been non-existent. It's been clear that Mark has very little interest in his child and Lulu wonders what has changed now and feels another pang of anxiety. But watching the scene around the table, she feels calmer. She drops her shoulders, takes a deep breath. How lucky she is to have such a supportive family.

Hal leans forward. 'He's picked it up very quickly,' he says, indicating the triumphant Ollie. 'He's already learning how to cheat.'

They both laugh and Lulu sips her tea. Of course she will tell them all about Mark getting in touch, but not before she's had a proper talk alone with Freddie. That will be difficult this evening but perhaps tomorrow they can slip away, make a plan. She takes another deep breath and settles into the corner of the sofa.

Fliss looks around at them all and thinks how delighted her grandmother, Freddy Chadwick, would be to see them all here, another generation finding sanctuary at The Keep. Though they are all uncertain how their lives will go forward yet, for this time, they are safe. Fliss feels so lucky to have them here. Her own children are far away. Jamie works at the Foreign Office and is in Dubai, and Bess and her husband and children are in Paris, but she's hoping that they might be home for Christmas if restrictions allow. She misses them all so much, and facetiming is better than nothing, but how she longs to see them, to hug them.

'Granny, it's your turn.' Ollie is tugging at her arm and she smiles down at him and picks up her cards.

CHAPTER EIGHT

Ed is walking in the gardens at Dartington Hall. Freddie and Lulu brought him here to have coffee at the Green Table café, reminding him of old times when he used to visit before he went to the States. He likes it here, and often comes on fine days to buy a takeaway coffee and sit in the sunshine. Now, as he walks, his mind is locked on to the secret he carries with him, his longing to be free from it and his cowardice, which makes freedom almost impossible.

He is barely aware of the beauty around him: the courtyard and medieval hall, the gardens in their late autumn glory revealing breathtaking views across the distant countryside. He's thinking of that latest text.

I shall find you, Ed. You can run but you can't hide. x

And even as he rounds the path that leads to the statue of Flora, he sees him. Tall, short dark hair, he is putting an offering of a large bronze-coloured leaf on the pedestal at Flora's feet. He turns before Ed can move and he smiles, holds out a hand as one might to a frightened animal.

'Don't look so surprised,' he says. 'You told me about your family in happier days so it wasn't too hard to find you. Chadwick is quite a big name round here. I must admit, though, that this is a lucky strike. I'm staying at the Hall. Very comfortable. The food's good.'

Automatically, Ed stretches out his hand and it's taken and held firmly.

'Xander,' he says. 'It's just . . . I didn't know how . . .'

Then he is being held and he feels weak with relief, with happiness.

'You always were a fool,' says Xander, releasing him. 'People are coming. Let's walk.'

They climb the steps and walk quickly across the grass to the temple that stands beneath the trees, looking out across the hills. They sit together on the wooden bench and Xander looks at him again and begins to laugh.

'Only you, Ed,' he says. 'Why didn't you let me know you were home?'

Ed shakes his head, staring down the grassy slope, hands clasped between his knees.

'Too ashamed,' he says. 'I was such a bloody fool. I bankrupted my mother with my ill-judged investments, let everybody down and ran away.'

Xander sighs. 'How long have we been friends? What age were we when we were choristers at Salisbury? Come on, Ed. This is me. I'm not going to let you hide any longer. You know that, don't you?'

Ed nods slowly. 'I do know it and I don't want to hide. But you said it yourself. Chadwick is a big name around here and it's going to be very hard to announce to my father and Fliss, not to mention the rest of my cousins, that I'm gay.'

He tries to imagine the scene, his father's reaction, Freddie's face, and all his old fear returns.

Xander touches his arm. 'I get it, Ed. I really do. But you can't keep running, and this is the twenty-first century. It's not a big deal any more. At least, it shouldn't be. And I'm here waiting for you.'

Ed tries to imagine the wonderful feeling of telling the truth, of being free of this dead weight, of taking Xander to meet his family, but it's almost too much: it's been so long.

'Come on,' says Xander. 'Let's go and grab a takeaway coffee from the Green Table and stroll around a bit.'

He leans across, kisses Ed lightly on the cheek, then they get up and walk away together.

Lulu and Freddie are driving up on to the moor. Out past Buckfast Abbey, through Hembury Woods, and up on to Holne Moor. In the back of Freddie's car, Honey sits up, looking expectantly through the window. She knows this road.

'I'm quite glad that Ed didn't want to come,' says Lulu. 'I just wanted this to be you and me so that we could talk about Mark.'

'So did I,' answers Freddie, as they bump over the cattle grid on to the moor. 'The person in the back can't hear properly and the front-seat passenger has to keep translating. Anyway, I think he's got something on his mind and needs some headspace.'

Lulu stares out at the spaces of gold and brown and rust: in the sunlight the dead bracken seems to be on fire and the distant tors are only just defined, blue-grey shapes against the brighter blue of the clear sky. There are sheep like white boulders grazing, and a group of ponies prance and kick up their heels, then stand still to watch the car pass by. Freddie drives slowly so that he too might enjoy the scene, then backs into the little space that was once part of a quarry and switches off the engine. The leat runs here, and hawthorn trees, bowed and shaped by the westerly winds, stand just above the quarry.

'This is Mum's favourite place,' Lulu says. 'She and Dad got engaged up here somewhere.'

'I think I remember her telling me that,' says Freddie. 'Good spot for it. Let's give Honey a walk before she breaks the window.'

'It's great that the choir is rehearsing again,' he says, as they free Honey and she races ahead beside the leat. 'They've got a Christmas production coming up at Dartington and Dad's just full of it.'

'Oh,' says Lulu, 'so that explains his high spirits. He seems to be particularly jolly just recently.'

'He's missed singing,' says Freddie. 'So come on. What's bugging you about Mark's email? It's not as if you're not in touch. Not that often, I know, but it's not quite out of the blue, is it?'

Lulu hunches herself into her jacket. It's not cold but there's a cool breeze.

'No,' she answers slowly, 'but there's something a bit different about this one. He says he's looking forward to seeing us. That it's been too long, and he's asking if he can stay, which is just not on. I simply couldn't cope with it. The trouble is that him being in the Netherlands, plus Covid, has made it very easy for him not to visit. It hasn't seemed to bother him at all till now, but suddenly there's this keenness. Ollie was only three when he left and he barely remembers him.'

'Are you really saying that you think Mark is regretting his decision and wants to come back?'

'Yes. No. Oh, I don't know.' Lulu sounds stressed. 'It's just a bit weird, that's all. And you know Mark. He's just so strong-willed. He always does it his way.'

'Well, that's in the past,' says Freddie firmly. 'You're no longer together, he can't insist he stays at The Keep, and although he must have reasonable access to Ollie there's absolutely no way he can force his way back into your life.'

'What if he should want to take Ollie to the Netherlands?' she asks, her voice full of fear.

Freddie snorts derisively. 'The courts would definitely have something to say about that. And so, I imagine, would Anneke. If he's regretting his decision that's his problem, not yours. What's he actually saying?'

'Stuff about missing us, and catching up with Ollie, especially with Christmas coming up. Just stuff, really. But he wants to make a plan and if I try to put him off he might just turn up anyway.'

'That would be a very stupid thing to do. Don't let him bully you, Lu.'

'But I can't refuse to let him see Ollie.'

'No, but we'll all be around when he does. You don't have to be frightened of him.'

'It's not so much frightened, it's that old thing of him making me feel inadequate.'

'It's called bullying,' says Freddie. 'You're not inadequate. You're running a successful business and raising a happy, well-balanced child. We'll plan a reply and take it from there.' He puts his arm around her shoulders and gives her a quick hug. 'Come on, let's catch Honey up.'

Lulu nods. She takes a calming breath, and follows him along the leat.

Clarissa is in Bayards Kitchen, the Cider Press coffee shop, seated on one of the long benches, when Susanna and Fliss come in. She sees them at once, waves delightedly, so that they are unable to turn and make a quick exit.

They order coffee and then join her, trying to appear as pleased to see her as she is to see them.

'This is really nice,' she says, as they sit down and take off their masks. 'I haven't seen you for ages. How are you both?'

'Fine,' answers Fliss. 'We're all absolutely fine. How about you and Ralph?'

'Well, he's busy as usual.' Clarissa makes a disgruntled face. 'I was hoping he might come with me this morning but someone phoned about some charity event and off he went.'

'All those good works,' says Fliss, sighing sympathetically.

'Well, it keeps him busy, I suppose.' She glances at Susanna. 'How's Gus? I saw him in Totnes the other day, in one of the art galleries. I nearly went in to say hi, but he was having such a good time with one of the assistants, I decided not to intrude.'

To Fliss's surprise, Susanna makes no retort, but she looks almost upset, and it's Fliss who says: 'He's really enjoying being able to sing again. Lots of the choir members work in the town. Gus knows everyone.'

'Yes,' agrees Susanna, who seems to have

pulled herself together. 'That's true. They've got a big event coming up in the Hall and they're all so excited about it. It's so good to have all these things happening after lockdown.'

Clarissa seems chagrined by this response and they talk about other things, whilst from time to time she hints that a Christmas get-together would be such fun. At last, to their relief, she gets up to go.

Fliss looks at her sister. 'So what's all that about?' she asks. 'You looked a bit odd when she was talking about Gus.'

Susanna sits for a moment staring down at her coffee.

'She'd already told me a few weeks ago that she saw Gus here with a pretty young woman. Then the next time I saw her I was here, having bumped into Hal, so we came in for some coffee. Clarissa was with Ralph. She asked about

Gus again, made a bit of a thing about it, all false concern and sympathy.'

Fliss looks puzzled. 'Hal didn't tell me that. I wonder why not.'

'Because I asked him not to,' says Susanna. 'It was silly and embarrassing, and I haven't been able to bring myself to ask Gus outright because it sounds . . .' – she shrugs – 'I don't know, kind of suspicious and weird, especially when I first told him what Clarissa said, and he just laughed and batted it away as an example of her being poisonous. But he's been so odd lately. A bit hyper, as if he's keeping a secret, and I don't quite know how to handle it. And now this. You're right, Gus knows loads of people, and he's always jokey, but this seems a bit different. Sorry. I shouldn't have asked Hal to keep it secret. That was wrong of me. It's just that I feel a fool.'

'It's OK,' says Fliss, but she feels a sense of

relief. There has been a caginess about Hal lately that she couldn't quite understand. 'I'm glad that you told me, though. Keeping secrets can be dangerous. Why don't you simply tell him what Clarissa has been hinting at and ask him straight out? I bet he'll roar with laughter and it's absolutely nothing. This isn't like you, Sooz. Or Gus. Don't let this stuff poison your relationship. It can if you're not careful.'

Susanna nods. She looks a bit tearful. 'I know you're right. I have wanted to, but it's just that I never quite know how to begin.'

'Just ask him, but make it a bit jokey. He knows what Clarissa's like.'

'I will.' Susanna seems to make up her mind. She sits up straighter and finishes her coffee.

'Good,' says Fliss. 'So where is Gus at the moment?'

'Sweeping up leaves,' answers Susanna. 'Well, he was when I left home.'

'OK, then,' says Fliss. 'Here's the plan. We go and buy some delicious bits in the deli and you and Gus come over for some lunch.'

'Sounds good to me,' her sister replies. 'But don't expect me to have asked him by then. I shall need to choose my moment.'

'Fine,' says Fliss, and they put on their masks and go out together.

CHAPTER NINE

Freddie beloved,

So here we are, almost the end of November and in Michael Mayne's book the month of November is the Dance of Faith. And how much we need faith. We are all pilgrims, but if we can keep trusting we are vouchsafed people for the journey. I've often found, when I look back, that when I think that I've been helping someone in fact it is he or she who has been strengthening me. Which is why dancing is so important: it's such a joyous thing, and 'how can we know the dancer from the dance?'

Since Chi-Meur opened to do weddings and even corporate events we are very busy. The setting here is so beautiful and all our guests love it. I have to admit that I rather enjoy it too. I like the bustle, though poor Clem is looking a little bit frazzled lately. Tilly remains her calm, cheerful self, although those two little ones are a handful and Jakey's having the usual teenager moments! So nice that we have young people living here.

Everyone sends their love to you.

It's time for Evening Prayer and I must go.

You are surrounded with love and prayers,

Sr Emily xx

Freddie sits beside the fire reading Sister Emily's letter, deep in thought, when he hears the knock at the door. He glances at his watch:

nearly nine o'clock, rather late for visitors. He gets up and opens the door. Ed is standing outside. He looks both anxious and excited, as if he is suppressing some deep emotions. Freddie tries not to look surprised but opens the door wider and steps aside.

'Come in,' he says. 'I thought you were going to the Cott with Fliss and Hal.'

'I changed my mind,' says Ed. 'Lulu and Ollie have gone to one of their sleepovers with Gus and Susanna so I've seized the moment. There's something I want to discuss with you, if you're OK with that.'

'Fine,' says Freddie. 'Glass of wine? I'm having a rather good Shiraz, compliments of Hal.'

'Yes,' says Ed quickly. 'Thank you. That might be good.' He looks around him at the fire, the bookshelves, the big table. 'It's really nice in here, isn't it?'

'I like it,' says Freddie, pouring a second glass. 'Come and sit down.'

They sit either side of the fire and Freddie wonders how to proceed, but Ed forestalls him.

'This is a bit weird,' he says. 'And I'm just going to go with it. The thing is, I'm gay. Nobody in the family knows because I've never been able to bring myself to tell them. After all those awful things happened, I just ran away but I don't think I can go on carrying this any longer.'

Freddie is taken completely off guard. He tries to take it in but is struggling, whilst Ed watches him anxiously.

'So Rebecca?' he asks at last. 'We all thought you were in a relationship with her.'

Ed shakes his head impatiently. 'She was a front. She's a very good friend and let me use her as a smokescreen. I was in a relationship but I just felt such a shit that I ran away from him too.'

Freddie takes a breath, prays for wisdom. 'But why did you feel that it needed to be a secret? There's no problem here, Ed.'

Ed stares at him. 'Seriously? You mean you're not shocked or . . . anything?'

'Why on earth should I be?' asks Freddie.

Ed pauses, then begins to laugh. 'I can't believe this. I'd worked myself up to all sorts of reaction – shock, disbelief, I don't know what.'

'Then you've misjudged me,' answers Freddie calmly, 'though I can imagine you might have some qualms about telling Hal, but only because you've hidden it so well from everybody.'

Ed takes a long swallow from his glass and Freddie can see that his hand is shaking slightly.

'So why now?' he asks. 'What was the trigger point?'

Ed stares at him and then laughs. 'I can see that I've totally underestimated you. Yes, you're right. The friend I was with before my flight to the States has discovered that I'm home and has been messaging me.'

'And?' Freddie asks after a long pause.

'He knew all about my family here and when I didn't respond he tracked me down. We met up by chance at Dartington. He's staying at the Hall.' Another silence. 'He wants us to be together again, but openly, and I want it too.'

'That's great,' says Freddie. He's very moved by Ed's disclosures, touched that he has been able to confide in him after all the difficulties there have been between them. 'So the next step is to tell the family. You haven't told me his name.'

'It's Alexander. Everyone calls him Xander.'

'Fine. So we need to make a plan. First tell Hal and Fliss and Lulu, then arrange a meeting. Is Xander still at the Hall?'

Ed nods. He looks alarmed. 'We can't all meet here. Not for the first time.'

Now it's Freddie who begins to laugh. 'I agree. Much too intimidating for a first meeting. It needs to be on neutral territory. But first you need to tell them. Do you need moral support for that?'

'Yes,' says Ed quickly. 'No. I don't know. Your reaction has taken me by surprise. I thought . . . well, I don't know what I thought, but I just need to take it in.'

'But don't leave it too long,' says Freddie. 'Don't lose your impetus and let anxiety back in. I'm very happy to meet Xander if you both think it might be helpful.'

'Yes,' says Ed. 'That might be a good idea. I'll talk to him. Thanks, Freddie.'

'Good,' says Freddie, 'but I definitely know what the next step is.' Ed looks puzzled. 'Another glass of wine. Drink up.'

113

After Ed has gone, Freddie sits staring into the fire, thinking, about Ed and about Sister Emily's letter. This will heal the ongoing rift between him and Ed; it explains Ed's brittleness, the veneer, the wariness. Something has changed and they will all be strengthened by it. Freddie feels a huge sense of peace. Perhaps, after all, he is learning to dance.

Supper is over, Ollie has settled down to sleep at last, and there is time to talk. And Lulu knows what the subject must be.

'Mark wants to come over,' she says abruptly. 'He says he wants to see us and he's asked if he can stay at The Keep. It's totally out of the blue and I don't know what to say.'

Her parents stare at her in surprise. 'When?' asks Gus.

'Before Christmas. And I just don't see how it can work.'

'He can't come to The Keep,' says Susanna, firmly. 'Good heavens, it's two years since he was here. I know Covid has caused problems but he could have come over this summer. And he's hardly ever in touch.'

'It sounds weird, as if things have gone a bit wrong for him, and suddenly he's all friendly,' says Lulu. 'But I can't stop him seeing Ollie.'

'But not necessarily at The Keep. He'll have to stay somewhere locally.'

'You know what he's like,' says Lulu. 'He's always so strong about what he wants to do.'

'He's a bully,' says Gus calmly. 'But you need have no fear. If he wants to come over and stay somewhere nearby, then Ollie can see him, but not alone. Ollie can hardly remember him, so you'd have to be there and one of us would be there with you, too.'

Susanna sits down on the sofa beside her and puts an arm around Lulu.

'I'd almost forgotten how intimidating he can be,' says Lulu, feeling as though she might cry. 'It's crazy but he just doesn't give in until he's got his way.'

'Well, he won't get it this time. Luckily, you're not on your own. He can't simply invite himself to The Keep. Don't panic, Lulu. He can't hurt you now.'

'It was all beginning to work out,' she says. 'I don't think Ollie cares any more, and I was getting over feeling so inadequate. And I've met this lovely guy who's just opened an art gallery in the town. I really thought we were moving on.'

'You are,' says Susanna. 'This is not going to stop you. I know you feel you must keep the channels open between him and Ollie, but there are ways to do that. It would help if Mark sent him a card or a present sometimes. He even forgot his birthday.'

'I know,' says Lulu miserably, 'but even so, I won't stop that kind of contact. I just don't get why he should want to meet up now, out of the blue, after two years.'

'I think you're right: something's gone wrong for him,' says Gus. 'He's fallen out with Anneke – perhaps she didn't like being bullied either – or maybe he's lost his job and this would be an easy route back. He's thinking you're at The Keep, why not him too? Or something like that. Anyway, it's not going to happen.'

'Shall we compose an answer?' suggests Susanna. 'Obviously it needs to be coming from you but we could help make it a bit punchy.'

She and Gus both watch Lulu, concerned and loving, and she smiles at them. 'Yes,' she says. 'Let's try that. Thanks. I feel much better now.'

Susanna gets up to make a cup of tea and Lulu breathes a sigh of relief. She knows it's silly to be so anxious but she simply couldn't bear that Mark's undermining her should begin all over again.

Gus smiles at her. 'We need some music,' he says.

Softly, the Andante from Shostakovich's Piano Concerto No. 2 drifts into the silence, and Lulu rests her head against the cushion and feels a sense of peace.

CHAPTER TEN

December

Ed and Xander are walking in the Dartington Hall gardens on a cold sunny day. The
dogwood burns crimson against the greys and
browns of the leafless shrubs, and coppery
leaves lie thick upon the ground.

'I still can't believe it,' says Xander. 'That
you've told them and everything is OK. It's
just utterly amazing.'

'It is,' says Ed. He wants to reach out and

grasp Xander's hand but feels that it's rather too public. 'Dad was silent for a moment, like I told you, and then he just got up and held out his arms to me. That's so not like Dad. I mean, we still shake hands when we meet up or when I go away. And he was just so completely understanding. He said, "It must have been so tough for you." I really thought I was going to cry. It was like Freddie. He was just so amazing, so understanding. I thought he'd be a bit, you know, sarky.'

'You've probably never seen the priest in him,' says Xander. 'I'm looking forward to meeting him. I have to say I feel a bit anxious about it now it's a reality, but it will be so good to get it over.'

'The whole question is where,' says Ed. 'I really can't decide where we'd all be most natural. Maybe Freddie is right and it should be on neutral ground. I'm afraid it might be a bit overwhelming otherwise.'

They've reached the Temple and they sit down on the bench, looking down the grassy slope to the field beyond.

'I love this place,' says Xander. 'In a weird way it feels like a homecoming. After all, I am a country boy. Listen, Ed. I've been thinking about the meeting and I've decided that I want to risk The Keep. After all, why not? It's much the easier thing to do than all sitting in a coffee shop or a pub. Shall we?'

Xander turns to look at him, and their hands meet on the bench between them and hold tightly.

'Right,' says Ed, feeling a surge of terror and elation. 'It'll be fine. We can do this.'

'Great,' says Xander, smiling at him. 'It's going to be so good, Ed. Trust me.'

'The crazy thing was,' says Hal to Fliss, 'that once he said it, everything just fell into place.

121

All that secrecy, withholding himself, was just self-protection.'

They're sitting in the kitchen, which is always kept warm by the Aga, and Honey is asleep in her basket.

'I know,' she answers him. 'I feel the same. Just a huge relief. I'm looking forward to meeting Xander. But I wonder what will happen next. Will they go back to London?'

'I asked Ed that this morning. Xander works in IT at the same company where Ed used to be, and he's working from home. He's suggesting that Ed should go and ask them for a job. Ed thought that if they agreed, he and Xander could stick around here for a bit with perhaps a weekly visit to London to check in. It seems like a lot of people work like that now.'

'That would be great,' says Fliss. 'We could really get to know Ed properly, and Xander too.'

Hal grins at her. 'Are you suggesting that he might come here?'

She laughs. 'We need to meet him first, but I must admit that the thought did just cross my mind, until they get settled.'

'Why not?' says Hal. 'Come one, come all. It's what The Keep does best.'

Susanna watches Gus through their open bedroom door. He's been elated and secretive all day and she can no longer hold back these foolish fears. She pushes the door wide open, and Gus springs round, shuts the wardrobe door behind him and stares at her guiltily.

'Gus,' she says, trying to keep her voice steady. 'I can't cope with all this secrecy and silence stuff any longer. What's it all about? Are you seeing another woman?'

His look of disbelief and amazement would have made her laugh on any other occasion, but not this time. He comes round the end of the bed and holds out his hands to her.

'Darling Sooz,' he says. 'Don't be silly. Whatever's brought this on?'

'Clarissa said she saw you up at Bayards with a young woman, and then again in one of the art galleries in Totnes. And you've been so strange. All secretive and kind of hyper.'

She sits down on the end of the bed, and he sits down beside her and takes her hands, holding them tightly. Unexpectedly she begins to cry and he puts his arms round her, his lips to her hair.

'OK,' he says. 'It was going to be a surprise but I see that I shall have to come clean.'

Letting her go, he gets up, walks round to the wardrobe and takes out a rectangular package.

'It was meant for you for Christmas, but I can't bear to see you like this.'

He tears away the packaging and holds it up.

It's a beautiful watercolour of a hawthorn tree, bent and shaped by winds, bright with scarlet berries, against a moorland background and a wild sky. Susanna stares at it, wiping her cheeks with her hands.

'It's our tree on Holne Moor,' he says gently. 'Where I proposed to you. I had to meet up with the artist, to show her photographs. Do you like it?'

And now she does cry, holding out her arms to him, as they fall together on to the bed, clutching each other tightly.

When Ed drives them under the gatehouse arch and pulls to a stop, Xander sits for a moment in silence.

'Wow,' he says softly. 'And double wow.'

Ed glances at him anxiously. 'Are you sure you're going to be OK?'

Xander nods, and they get out of the car, and

then Ed realizes that the front door is partly open, lights are on, and festive music is playing.

'Come on,' says Ed, puzzled.

He takes Xander's arm, pushes the door wide open and they go inside. The hall is full of noise and merriment. Hal and Freddie have brought in the Christmas tree. It stands tall in the corner, whilst Fliss, watching them, is holding the fairy lights in her hands, and Lulu and Ollie kneel before the boxes that contain the decorations. A log fire is burning in the huge hearth.

'Oh my God,' says Xander softly, beginning to smile.

Hal sees them and calls out. 'Good timing. Two more pairs of hands,' and suddenly everyone is laughing, talking, introducing themselves, and Ed is filled with a huge sense of gratitude and happiness. It's as if he's coming home for the first time. Xander is already part of the busy group. He turns to glance at Ed with a look of love and Ed joins them and all is well.

Freddie, seeing the look that passes between them, smiles to himself. He has his own reason to be cheerful. His latest letter from Chi-Meur was not from Sister Emily but from Clem.

. . . This is a cry for help, old friend. The retreat house is really doing well, but our parish is going into an interregnum just after Christmas and there will be no priest to assist me. Is there any chance you could come and help us? Bed and board, of course, and a small salary, but we'd all love to have you here and it would be saving my life . . .

Freddie's heart leaped with joy and gladness. His prayers were being answered. Now he looks around the hall. Ollie is already friends with

Xander and showing him the decorations, and Lulu looks so content. Mark has tested positive for Covid and can't leave the Netherlands, and for the moment the problem of his visit is shelved. Freddie gives thanks, and murmurs the prayer his great-uncle Theo always said at family gatherings: 'God bless us, every one.'

Ed stands at his bedroom window, looking down into the courtyard. He's watching Freddie and Lulu playing a ball game with Ollie when Xander's car appears under the arch of the gatehouse and they all go to greet him as he gets out. The gatehouse lights twinkle in the dusk and Ed can't wait for him and Xander to be there together, once Freddie has gone to be chaplain at Chi-Meur. The group in the courtyard are laughing as Xander bends to catch the ball that Ollie throws to him and Ed's heart is filled with happiness. He remembers driving in, a couple of months ago, looking around him, thinking: nothing has changed. Ed turns away from the window and goes down to join the party in the courtyard.

Everything has changed.

ACKNOWLEDGEMENTS

First and foremost, to my much-loved late husband Roddy, who persuaded me to write and thus to make me the following friends:

Cate Paterson, Clare Foss, the late Jane Morpeth, Yvonne Holland, Sue Fletcher, Susie Watts, Linda Evans, Patrick Janson-Smith, Larry Finlay, Bill Scott-Kerr, Kevin Redmond, Harriet Bourton, Francesca Best, Molly Crawford, Imogen Nelson, Vivien Thompson, Josh Benn, Marianne Issa El-Khoury, Helen Edwards, Chris Smale, Tom Hill, Hayley Barnes, Izzie

Ghaffari-Parker, Josh Crosley, Kiran Kataria, Fay Pafford, Kathleen Anderson, Tom Dunne, Marcia Markland, Hilary McMahon, Kim McArthur, Regina Hartig, Iris Gehrman, Christian Stuewe, Ulf Töregård, Ninni Töregård, Alis Friis Caspersen, Niels Gudbergsen, Anne Sondergaard, Elisabeth Strandgaard, Trine Maehl, Frederika von Traa, Karen Bikkel, Michelle Lapautre, Catherine Lapautre, Claire de Robespierre, Krista Kaer, Nike Davarinou, Louisa Zaoussi, Jill Hughes.

I would like to thank the illustrators of my books all over the world whose beautiful cover designs have given me so much joy.

I am very grateful to Bob Mann who gave me my first press review, to Annette Shaw at *Devon Life*, to Judi Spiers and all at Radio Devon. To Pat Abrehardt who arranged my very first signing party, and to all staff at the Harbour Bookshop in Kingsbridge. To Simon and Natasha at Bookstop, to Cliff and Martin at Totnes Bookshop, to Andrea at the Community Bookshop and the staff at Browser Bookshop in Dartmouth, as well as other local booksellers who have stocked and sold so many copies of my novels.

I have been constantly encouraged by messages from loyal readers, especially Marilyn Bertrand. Thank you all for your emails which have been such a joy to receive.

Love to my sisters Paula and Bridget, whose eagle eye prevented many mistakes, and to Pam Goddard, whose early read of my manuscripts was always invaluable.

Special thanks to Rick. Without your technical support and advice, it would have been very difficult for me to write my later novels.

Finally, very special thanks to my agent Dinah.

ABOUT THE AUTHOR

Marcia Willett's early life was devoted to the ballet, but her dreams of becoming a ballerina ended when she grew out of the classical proportions required. She had always loved books, and a family crisis made her take up a new career as a novelist – a decision she never regretted.

She lived in a beautiful and wild part of Devon, and her surroundings inspired many of her novels.

Marcia passed away in June 2022 after a period of ill health. She leaves behind a son and two grandchildren. *Christmas at the Keep* is her last book.